It's Raining

Danish Nursery Rhymes

A Margaret K. McElderry Book

AN ALADDIN BOOK
Atheneum

Said John Twaining

Translated and Illustrated by

N. M. Bodecker

RAAGEHUS
1922 1972

DANMARK

2 Öre

DANMARK

To Dagny Riis

Rosdal

Mr. Lem pr. Lemvig

Denmark

Søndagsbrev

PUBLISHED BY ATHENEUM
COPYRIGHT © 1973 BY N. M. BODECKER
ALL RIGHTS RESERVED
PUBLISHED SIMULTANEOUSLY IN CANADA BY
MCCLELLAND & STEWART, LTD.
MANUFACTURED IN THE UNITED STATES OF AMERICA BY
CONNECTICUT PRINTERS, HARTFORD
ISBN 0-689-70437-2
FIRST ALADDIN EDITION

"It's raining," said John Twaining

"Keep me dry!"
said John Rye.

"No I will not,"
said John Willmot.

"You must go!"
said John Slow.

"Go where?"
said John Square.

"To Jack Crowning,"
said John Browning.

"What for?"
said John Sore.

"Buy some coats!"
said John Oats.

"How many?"
said John Penny.

"Ten should do,"
said John Drew.

"Want to bet?" said John Wett.

Three little Guinea pigs
went to see the King.
One brought a rose;
one brought a ring;
one brought a turnip
to give to the King.

Two went back home
neither fatter
nor thinner.
One sat on the Queen's lap
and ate the King's dinner.

Little Miss Price
rode with her mice
over the ice.

Crack! went the ice.

Squeek! went the mice.

Home in her basket went little Miss Price.

Row, row, row
to Oyster Bay.
What sort of fish
shall we catch today?
Big fish,
small fish,
snook or snail,
yellow snapper,
triple tail,
herring
daring,
kipper
coarse,
or a trout
with applesauce?

Me and I and you
sailed a wooden shoe.

When we came to Connecticut,
the shoe was full of water, but

when we came to Spain,
it all ran out again!

On a green, green hill
I saw two rabbits come.
One he was a piper;
the other played a drum,
on a green, green hill in the morning.

A hunter shot the drummer;
the drummer lost his life.
The other little rabbit
now sadly plays his fife
on a green, green hill in the morning.

Little Jock Sander of Dee,
five little goslings had he.
He put them away for the night
and bid them sleep safely and tight.
But the hawk came to Dee;
he took the three!
The fox came too;
he took the two!
After this theft
how many were left?

The goose and the gander
and little Jock Sander!

There once was a King
who had three daughters.
The oldest he called
Sip!

The second he called
Sip sippernip!
But the youngest of all he called
Sip sippernip sip sirumsip!

Not far away lived another King
who had three sons.
The oldest was called
Skrat!

The second was called
Skrat skratterat!
But the youngest of all was called
Skrat skratterat skrat skrirumskrat!

Now by and by
the two Kings got together,
the King who had three daughters
and the King who had three sons,
and decided that their children
should marry.
And married they were!

Sip
got
Skrat

and
Sipsippernip got Skratskratterat
and
Sipsippernipsipsirumsip got Skratskratteratskratskrirumskrat. As simple as that!

Who
is knocking,
knock
knock
knock?
Charlie
Charlie
chuck
chuck
chuck!
Who
will open
up
up
up?
Peter
Peter
hop
hop
hop!

Pat-a-cake,
pat-a-cake,
what shall
we bake?
A big
birthday cake?
A pin cake,
a pancake,
a thin cake,
a sand cake?
Up it goes
and down
it comes,
the cake
is in the fire.

Two cats were sitting in a tree,
kritte vitte vit bom bom,
a cat called Lew,
a cat called Lee,
kritte vitte vit bom bom.
"Now follow me,"
said Lew to Lee,
kritte vitte vitte vitte vit bom bom,
for I no longer like this tree,
kritte vitte vit bom bom!

So Lew and Lee
climbed down the tree,
kritte vitte vit bom bom.
Once down the tree
to Lew said Lee,
kritte vitte vit bom bom,
"Oh, Lew, I rather liked that tree!"
kritte vitte vitte vitte vit bom bom.
So Lew and Lee climbed up the tree,
Kritte vitte vit bom bom!

My little	good 'un,	and one little piggie	Five little piggies
dad	bad 'un,	who was	had
had	gay 'un,	mad	my little
five little piggies:	sad 'un,	mad mad!	dad.

"Squire McGuire,
how much is your lyre?"

"A dollar, McDoo,
since the strings are quite new.

"If you want it more lavish,
go to McTavish.

"If you want it just plain,
you must go to McLain!"

Quail
snail
tattletale,
making up a story!

Grouse
louse
blabbermouth,
tomorrow you'll be sorry!